THE ARRANGEMENT

Vol. 12

H.M. Ward

www.SexyAwesomeBooks.com

Laree Bailey Press

COPYRIGHT

THE ARRANGEMENT

Vol. 12

CHAPTER 1

This can't be happening. The phrase repeats over and over again in my mind as my skin prickles with dread. There's so much blood on the carpet, seeping out from under the sheet. The crushed black bead did her no good.

The cop doesn't see me yet. Any second he'll turn around and I have no idea what I'll say. The floor isn't closed off. I don't know why and I don't care. Sean is going to kill me for coming back up here, but I can't leave Mel like this. My heart is stuck in my throat, forming a giant knot that won't go away no matter how hard I swallow.

A noise startles me out of my trance and I glance at the purse, clutched tightly in my hands. The cop turns and sees me. Sean's voice is spilling from within the room and I only take notice when it stops. He knows I'm here. The ring tone clangs again before I realize what it means. My shoulders stiffen and I dig through my bag, trying to find the phone as fast as possible.

"You shouldn't be up here, miss." The cop says, and starts to walk toward me.

My smile is weak, timid almost. "I'm sorry, I—" I stop talking and look at the picture on my screen. Ice drips down my spine and pools in my stomach. Mel's murderer stole her phone and is calling me. The crass stripper ring tone blares again and I swipe the button to accept the call. "Hello?"

The cop walks toward me as I stand still, shivering. I expect to hear a male's voice, someone sick and twisted. He's going to say something horrible, but what I hear shocks me even more.

"Avery? Are you listening to me? Get the fuck out of there! Now!" It's Mel. My hands start shaking and I suck in a ragged breath.

"Mel—?" My voice catches in the back of my throat as my skin gets covered in a new wave of gooseflesh.

"Miss, this floor is closed." The cop talks at the same time as Mel. The man is wearing his uniform, and he has that seriously displeased look policemen wear when they've seen too much. My God, what happened in that room while Sean and I were downstairs?

"Avery. Leave. Now." Her words come out staccato, emphasizing each one so that it sinks in.

I'm still in shock, with a haze hanging over me, where I can barely think. "Where are you?"

Mel doesn't tell me. "You're not listening. Something happened and I did what I had to do. Get the hell out of there. I wouldn't have even called, but the thing is, I think she was after you, not me. Be safe. Call me if you need help." The line goes dead.

Swallowing hard, I place my phone in my purse and nod at no one. The cop thinks I'm nodding at him and lifts his hand toward the elevator banks. At that moment, Sean peeks out from the doorway. I turn back and our eyes lock, but neither of us speaks. He doesn't want me involved in this, but I don't know if it can be avoided.

"Mr. Ferro," says a deep voice from within the room, "we're not done here."

Sean glances back at the man and then to me. "One moment." Sean walks down the hallway toward me with swift, determined, strides. He stops a step from me, like we're acquaintances and hands me a card. "I'll be a little bit. Meet me here. I have to go out to Long Island to take care of something, after this gets settled." His eyes are liquid blue and filled with worry. He blinks it away and his gaze once again turns to steel.

A large detective wearing a poorly fitting blue suit steps into the hallway. "Mr. Ferro, we're not done." The man has jowls that are cartoonish. He's way past his prime, with a belly that hangs over his belt, and bags under his eyes. There's a large nose in the center of his face that reminds me of Gabe. The man looks up at me and then glances at Sean. "Who's this?"

Sean speaks before I have a chance to answer. "A friend. She wasn't up here when this happened."

The uniformed cop looks at me with added interest. The detective asks, "Then, where were you?"

I feel nervous with all their eyes on me and spit out the truth. "In the dining room, downstairs."

The detective walks toward me. "What's your name, sweetheart?" I tell him and he asks if I've been up here tonight. I omit the fact that I was up here with Mel earlier and talk about dinner. "What are you doing here, now?"

"I came to see Mr. Ferro." It's the truth and I look too innocent or naïve to them. They both disregard me after a few more questions, but then he asks for the paper Sean handed me. "Let me see it and you can go."

I don't want to show him, but I do. Holding the business card between two fingers, I lift it up so he can read it. The man grunts and shakes his head. "A strip club? He handed you a card for a strip club?"

I shrug and smile bashfully, like Sean and I are into kinky things. The cop inhales suddenly, and it's way too loud. My outfit screams proper, refined, and totally average, but the card throws him off. The cop asks, "Why'd he give it to you?"

I smile, and look at the carpet and say the first lie I can conjure. "I was looking for a place to have a bachelorette party. He said he knew this place."

The cop glances at my ring, and then at Sean who has a stoic expression and doesn't speak. Sean's hands are in his pockets, as if he's bored. The two police officers look at one another, as if they know they're missing something, but neither is sure what. It seems like it lines up, thank God. The last thing I need is for them to think I'm lying.

Sean finally lets out an irritated sound and says, "Gentlemen, can we please figure out who killed the woman in my room so I can get on with business?"

Holy fuck, his voice is cold. Sean makes the woman's death sound like an inconvenience on the same level as missing a train. The words send a shiver down my spine. Sean tips his head toward me—bidding me good night—turns on his heel, and heads back to the room. I watch him disappear behind the door, and pass that lifeless body. He doesn't flinch, or look down at her. There's no indication that he's upset in any way, which is really disturbing. The thing is, I know this is the way he acts when he has his guard up. Sean becomes a rock, this stoic man completely devoid of emotion. It's damning because he looks like a freaking sociopath.

At that moment, I wonder what's really going through his mind, and if he's angry, worried, or what. That woman is dead. Someone killed her and I don't think Sean knows any more about it than I do.

My mouth feels like it has weights hanging from the corners, making me frown. Staring at her dead hand, I ask,

"Who is she?" My voice warbles slightly as my hand lifts to my heart.

I gawk at the sheet, thinking everything and nothing. It's one of those weird moments where so many thoughts and fears are rushing through my mind that I can't see any of them. They're a squall of storms, devastating and powerful, reminding me that life is fleeting, as if I didn't already know.

I can't help it, I start shaking. My reaction is involuntary, and I have no idea how Sean can compartmentalize so well that he could step over her without showing any concern. I'm all emotion, and the turmoil within me is gaining speed, ripping away the small fraction of control that remains. My stomach twists and my throat constricts as the contents of my stomach threaten to come up. I cover my mouth and look away as sweat beads across my forehead.

The detective swears, before saying, "Get her out of here before she's sick." The cop nods and takes my elbow, and turns me toward the elevators as his boss walks back toward Sean. There are more people in the room. I hear their voices, but never saw their faces.

The elevator chimes and the doors slide open. The cop walks me inside and tells me to hold the rail, before pressing the button for the lobby. His dark gaze lifts and meets my pale, sweaty face. He shoots me a look of pity and smiles. "Don't worry, miss. It's not someone you would know. The woman was a prostitute. Go down to the bar and ask for a lemon. Suck on it and the queasy feeling will settle."

All I can do is nod. The doors slip shut and I'm alone.

CHAPTER 2

Time passes strangely in the next few moments. It feels like I'm in my body and watching from above at the same time. My steps from the elevator feel heavy and light. Contradictions flood me and I have no idea why. The cop's words ring in my ear, his raspy, deep voice continues like a never ending echo. "The woman was a prostitute."

I hear the sound of my heels clicking on the marble floor and continue quickly toward the bar. I don't have any alcohol wipes in my purse and my throat is too tight. Add to that the torrent in my stomach and if I don't get a lemon in the next two seconds, I'm going to lose it.

The people around me register as noise. I don't know anyone, I don't see anyone. I'm engulfed in my own personal hell that hovers around me like a cloud. As I step into the bar, a hand lands on the crook of my arm and yanks.

My reaction is instant. I whirl around with my fist already balled, throwing all my weight into the swing with my arm. The man catches my fist in his palm and holds it for a second.

"Avery, calm down. Where the hell did you go? I need to get you out of here." It's Gabe. I can't calm down enough to let out a sigh of relief. My entire body is strung tight and ready to pop.

I nod at him and he lowers my arm to my side. "Come on. Back to Black's before this mess gets bigger."

I snap out of my stupor and shake my head. "No, I need to go here." I hold up Sean's card and Gabe plucks it from my fingers.

People move about us, murmuring about the dead woman in the Ferro suite. I hear their voices, and can't block them out. "The man is a monster. They should just shoot him," one woman says sternly as she walks by in a hurry.

A man passing in the other direction is grinning deviously, "That's one way to get out of paying, huh? I always heard Ferro was a cheap bastard."

The comments barrage me, and don't stop. Each wave of insults is worse than the last. They hate him—everyone thinks he did it and Sean wasn't even in the room.

My lips press together in a twitchy way as I regain my composure enough to act. I spin on my heel to grab the asshole's shoulder and tell him off, but Gabe sees the movement and stops me before I have the chance.

His hands land on my waist and he yanks me away. I want to turn and claw his face off. I'm fuming. It feels like someone ripped me open from sternum to navel, and I can't tell if I want to fight back or lay down and cry. "Stop it, Miss Stanz. Do not draw more attention to yourself." Gabe hisses in my ear. "I'll take you to this place, if this is where you want to go, but we leave now. No comments. You don't know a damn thing, and if you tackle someone, I swear to God that I'll taser your ass and throw you in the trunk. Got it?" The old guy is puffed up like he means business.

Attacking assholes won't help Sean, so I nod. I didn't expect Gabe to comply so easily, but I'm not about to ask questions. He releases me, I follow him out a side door, and we shove past a mob of people trying to get inside. Reporters look at us and some flashes go off, but then they realize that we're nobodies and drop their cameras to their sides. The chatter begins again and I hear more of the same. They're condemning Sean and growing into a frenzy. I hear someone say that Amanda's death was unnecessary and now this.

I turn and look at the guy. We make eye contact, but Gabe holds onto my arm and pulls me away. I don't speak, but I wonder—what kind of life would Sean have had if Amanda hadn't killed herself and taken his only child? His personal hell is expanding, and this event will make it so much worse.

After Gabe deposits me in the back seat, he jumps in the limo, and we're off. We make it through the Brooklyn-Battery Tunnel and back onto Long Island quickly. I stare out the window, watching lights blur by, lost in thought.

Gabe finally speaks up, "Where were you?"

Glancing up at the mirror, I look into his old eyes. "Not in the room, if that's what you're asking. I didn't do this and neither did Sean. We were in the restaurant."

He nods and grips the steering wheel tighter. "I noticed the rock on your finger. People saw you two?"

"Yeah, they saw us." My voice is soft and my shoulders finally relax. I feel like a deflating balloon that was smacked too many times.

"Good, then this shouldn't lead back to Black."

I glance up at him and know—call it a gut instinct—that he's wrong. This will lead back to Miss Black, and possibly everyone else. My lips part as my gaze narrows. The words don't come out of my mouth, but he watches me. The old guy sees everything and I'm still an open book, unable to hide the thoughts rushing through my mind. The worry line between his eyebrows deepens. "Spit it out, kid. You're thinking something, and if it affects all of us, you have to spit it out."

I only say two words, but he knows what I mean. "The bracelet."

CHAPTER 3

Gabe swallows so hard that I can hear it from the back seat. The man actually turns his head to look at me. "She crushed the black stone?" After our eyes lock, both wide with worry, I nod once. "Holy fuck."

Gabe whips his head back around and accelerates, bobbing and weaving through traffic like his ass is on fire. He grumbles things to himself, but he doesn't turn back toward Black's. Instead, he keeps his word and drives me to the strip club on Long Island where I'm supposed to meet Sean later.

I slump back into the seat and think of the ramifications of the broken bead and why Gabe didn't know it was crushed. When I crushed the stone, he was there, smashing through the door and then promptly pummeling Henry Thomas into the floor. My heart starts to race again. I never thought of having a faulty transmitter in my bracelet. Is that what happened to Mel? My God. I can't imagine what would have happened if I crushed the stone and Gabe didn't show up the night Henry went nuts. The thought sends a shiver down my spine and for once I keep my face expressionless as my mind drifts through the consequences.

If Gabe didn't show up and I was on my own, what would I do? The thought never occurred to me. I had this sense of security, that if anything went screwy all I had to do was crush that stone and help would arrive. It never felt like I was on my own, left to my own devices to defend myself, but it seems like that's exactly what happened to Mel.

What would Mel do if help didn't come? She held her own on the streets long before I ever met her. The attitude she projects says *don't screw with me*, so I can't imagine who would—or why. It makes no sense. When Sean and I left, Mel was ordering a buffet from the room service menu. How'd she go from pigging out to fleeing, leaving behind a dead body on the floor?

I see the lifeless curled fingers poking out from under the sheet in my mind. I remember the massive amount of blood that soaked into the carpet around her. What happened? Better yet, who was she? Why was she there and who killed her?

'Fuck' is the right expression. We're all screwed if this gets traced back to Black. I glance up at Gabe and try to keep my thoughts off my face. "Why didn't her transmitter work?"

Gabe's jaw is locked tight as he shifts his lower jaw from side to side. He's livid, but I'm not certain of the reason. It could be fear of exposure or something worse. God, what could be worse? He lets out a huff of air and inhales again before looking in the mirror at me. "No clue." That's all he says before locking his jaw again.

The hairs on the back of my neck prickle as he looks away. It's an ominous feeling and I know he's lying to me. There's more going on than I'm aware of, a lot more.

We exit the expressway and drive down some side streets until we stop in front of a shack. Okay, calling the strip club a shack is kind. It's just scary looking, complete with a neglected façade and a decaying parking lot that's turning to dust.

Gabe's expression changes into a look of concern. "You sure this is where Mr. Ferro wanted you to go?"

I nod, gaping at the building with the same dumbfounded expression. "Yes."

"It looks like the place is closed."

Yeah, it does. There are only a few cars in the parking lot and the sign on the door is flipped to CLOSED. What the hell is Sean thinking? There's only one way to find out. I move before Gabe snaps out of it, and open my door. My heels hit the gravel and I nearly twist my ankle, but I recover and straighten.

Gabe rushes toward me, and closes my door. We both stand there, shoulder to shoulder, and stare at the old building. "I think I should walk you inside."

I think that he should, too. Honestly, the place creeps the crackers out of me, but Sean wouldn't have sent me here if it wasn't safe. My gaze drifts to the ring on my finger, and I know without a doubt that Sean asked me to come here to keep me safe. Although I want Gabe to walk me in, I don't know what secrets Sean has hidden here and I don't want to cause more trouble. "It's okay, I'll be fine. You can go back to Black's."

The old guy eyes me like I have a spine of steel and nods. He scratches his scruffy cheek and looks at the car. "I'll tell Black that I didn't find you—that you were already gone."

"But what about the bracelet?" She'll see that I was in the limo.

He shrugs. "I'll make something up."

I reach toward him and squeeze his forearm. It's the closest thing to a hug that I can offer without him taking my head off. Well, not that I think Gabe would hurt me, but I want to reassure him in some way and it seems like the right gesture.

"Be careful. I don't know what's going on, but this feels wrong." Gabe glances at my hand and then up at my face. He has the perpetual frown he always wears and pats the top of my hand. "Trust your gut, kid." That's all he says before turning away. He doesn't wait for me to go inside before driving away.

I watch the red tail lights disappear down the street and stand there, alone, staring at the door to the strip club. I better head inside and find out why Sean sent me here.

CHAPTER 4

My heart pounds a little faster as I cross the parking lot. The wind rustles the barren branches of the trees at the back of the building, making me look in the shadows for ominous figures. I'd planned on going inside and sitting in the back, blending in amongst the other patrons as much as possible, and waiting for Sean. It's late and the place is empty, closed, so that plan's tossed. When I walk inside, assuming the door is unlocked, everyone is going to look at me and wonder what the hell I'm doing here.

I need to grow some balls. I swear, it seems like everything scares me lately. Before I reach the door, my phone buzzes. I glance at the screen. It's Mel.

"Where are you?" I snap before she has a chance to say anything else.

"Driving in circles. Where are you?" Mel's voice doesn't have the cool composure that she's known for, which worries me.

I tell her where I am. "Get your ass out here now." Mel agrees and the line goes dead. Pressing my fingers to my temples, I try to fight off the compulsion to bang my head into the wall. Fuck it. I bang my forehead against the door and let the cold metal freeze my brain.

What have I done? How did I get mixed up with all this shit? I'm enough of an emotional basket-case without dead bodies. I shut my eyes and take a deep breath, intending to steady myself to push open the door and waltz inside like I belong in this place, but that doesn't happen.

Within a moment of resting my head on the door, it's yanked open and I fall forward. My body slams into some guy.

Strong arms catch me and for a second all I can see is a dark dress shirt with the top buttons undone, and a silver ring hanging around his neck. The guy straightens me up, holding me by my shoulders. His lips twist into a sexy smirk. "You okay?"

I finally get a look at his face and freeze. Holy shit, is that Trystan Scott? The guy is a legend. He's the biggest rock star around, and the guy is standing in front of me. My eyes widen and I manage to blink once. It can't be him. No way. This has to be a double, or some sort of impersonator, for the club.

A dorky smile crosses my mouth and I tuck my hair behind my ear. "Yeah, I'm fine. Sean Ferro told me to come out here—"

The guy's smile vanishes and he looks me over again. "You know Sean?" I nod. "And you willingly came here to see him?" He glances past me like there might be a militia hidden in the parking lot, holding me here at gunpoint.

I nearly laugh. He knows Sean, that much is certain, because he doesn't like him at all. I poke the guy in the chest and get in his face. Today's been too long to deal with this twerp. "Listen, Trystan impersonator, I don't have to tell you a damn thing. Now let me inside before I get mugged and Sean kills you and buries you out back."

The smirk returns, but brighter this time. He's trying not to laugh. "Uh, yeah, first things first—I'm not afraid of Sean Ferro, and second—I *am* Trystan Scott." He glances down at my finger, which is still pressed into his chest, like I intend on kicking his ass myself, before looking back up into my face.

A stupid expression is frozen on my lips and suddenly I can't speak. My eyes slowly widen as I recognize the dimples, the scar, and the distinct traits of the rock star. His father beat the shit out of him when he was younger and the proof is forever on his skin. I'm caught between looking like an asshole and a crazy woman. Fuck. I need to pick one and just go with it. I drop my finger and place my hands on my hips and tilt my head at him. "Why would Sean send me to you, if you hate him?"

Trystan shrugs—I can't believe it's really him. This is totally weird. "No idea.

He does a lot of illogical shit that only makes sense in his twisted mind." He lets his eyes rove over me once and spots the ring on my finger. His jaw drops as he points toward my hand. "No fucking way. Is that from Ferro?"

Now I feel naked. The way this guy looks at me, with such utter amazement, is unsettling. I cover my engagement ring with my hand. "Yes."

Something shifts and the amused smile returns. "Now you have to come in." I glance up at him and wonder what made him drop his guard, but he clearly has. Instead of being suspicious of me, he seems to like me. The change happened in a snap.

"I don't get it." Looking into those icy blue eyes, I can see that Trystan knows what I'm asking.

"Anyone that is capable of taming Sean Ferro is a force to behold. You've captured my attention, Future-Mrs. Ferro, which is difficult to do." Trystan pushes the door open, extending his arm, and ushers me inside.

CHAPTER 5

The interior is as dreary as the outside. Trystan has an amazed look on his face and occasionally glances at me out of the corner of his eye. I spot someone—a woman with long hair—sitting at a table alone in front of the stage. Her back is curved and she's leaning heavily on her elbows.

Trystan walks directly toward her. "Hey, Sidney, look who I found on the front porch—the future Mrs. Sean Ferro." He grins at me and throws himself into a seat across from the woman.

It's not until she turns around that I recognize her. Some of the anguish in my chest dissipates and I rush at her with a huge smile. "Oh my God! It's you!"

Sidney laughs and hugs me back. "Avery, it's so good to see you!"

"Awh, a reunion. If I'd known, I would have brought dip." Trystan leans back in his chair and kicks his feet up onto the table. He's wearing an old pair of black Chucks. Blue argyle socks peek out from beneath his dark jeans. The hem is shredded in places, along with one of the knees. That silver ring around his neck is out of sight, but the chain is still visible.

Sidney snaps at him as she releases me. "Shut up, Trystan. Anyone that's had to put up with Sean—"

He drops his feet to the ground, leans forward and grabs my hand, thrusting it toward Sidney so she can see my ring. "No, not put up, tamed—this chick tamed the jackass known as Sean Ferro."

Sidney's jaw drops and she takes my hand from Trystan and then looks up into my face. "Oh my God! He asked you to marry him?"

I can't help it. For a moment, I forget about all the horrible things that have happened and smile at her. "Yes, he did."

"When?"

"Tonight."

Sidney squeals and jumps up and down. Since she's holding my hand, I jump with her. Trystan has his arms folded over his chest and watches us. There's no one else around, but I hear voices. I glance about and ask her, "Why are you here?"

"Because Peter's here. His brother bought this place and shouldn't have—at least that's what Pete said—so Sean did something to make it like it never happened. Jonathan just has to sign some papers, but he doesn't want to."

We step apart and I look over at Trystan, not understanding why he's here. He leans his chair back on two legs and raises a finger, "Best friend of the accused. And for the record, I think Jon should do whatever the fuck he wants. God knows Sean does."

"So, you know Sean?" I ask. From the way Trystan speaks, it sounds like they've met more than once.

He glances up at me from under those dark eyebrows and nods. "Yup. He hates my guts." My lips part to say that can't possibly be true, but Trystan smiles and shakes his head, making his long, dark hair fall in his eyes.

He pushes it back and lets the legs of his chair slam down. "It's okay, the feeling is mutual. You don't have to apologize for him. It's just the way things are, besides, you impressed the hell out of me. Anyone that can domesticate Sean Ferro deserves a statue and a holiday named after them." Trystan jumps up and crosses the room to the bar, grabbing shot glasses, and a bottle of amber liquid. He walks it over to our table and sets it down. "Let's celebrate."

Sidney looks back at the closed door at the back of the room. "But, they could be done at any moment."

Trystan shakes his head. "Nah, they're going to be in there for a while. Cassie's back there, and there's no way in hell that Jon is going to sign the papers. I'll be shocked if he caves in, especially in front of her. It's going to be a long night. Drink up." Trystan pours three shots and slides glasses towards Sidney and me.

"To the impossible." He holds up his drink, waiting for us to clink his glass.

Fuck it. God knows I could use a drink. My nerves are frayed beyond belief and if I think too much, I'm going to turn into a weeping mess. I pluck the glass from the table and look over at Sidney, knowing that she doesn't drink very much. "Knock it back fast."

Sidney sucks in way too much air, and lifts the glass. She's nervous. The three of us tap our shot glasses together and throw back the liquor. Trystan acts like it's water and gulps it, expressionless. My nose scrunches up as the liquor burns its way down my throat, and poor Sidney doesn't slam it back fast enough. The alcohol must have grabbed her tonsils, because she makes the most god-awful face and chokes, but somehow the little cup is empty. She hacks up a lung as I pat her back.

When Sidney looks up at me, she's laughing. "Yeah, I tried to sip it." The way she acts brings back memories of the first time I met her. There's something about

Peter's fiancée that is so sweet and innocent. I envy her in that moment and assume she's had an easy life, but the thought stumbles. There's been something dark there, too—a reason why Peter asked Sean for help, and it had something to do with Sidney.

Trystan pushes his hair out of his face and pours another round. "You guys are going to be sisters-in-law, which makes me your new best-friend-in-law." He glances at me and pushes my drink my way, as his lips take on the amused smirk that he wore at the door. "So, tell me, how'd you get Sean Ferro wrapped around your little finger?" That's when things start to get interesting.

CHAPTER 6

I don't plan on telling Trystan my occupation, but nothing goes as planned tonight. We sit around the table and talk about everything and anything. It's strange, I barely know these people, but it doesn't feel that way. I slump back into my chair and stare at the stage with another drink in my hand. "Why would Sean's little brother buy this place?"

Trystan is leaning back on his chair, with his feet on the table again, staring at the bottom of an empty glass. The corner of his mouth tugs up on one side, reminding me of a kid with a kaleidoscope. "Why does any guy do something stupid?"

"For a woman." Sidney dips her finger into her drink and lets the drop fall on her tongue before making a face.

Trystan nods at her. "Damn right, but I worry about him. This is the girl that tore Jon to shreds and he's risking everything for her. She seems sincere enough, but he thought she was the real deal last time too. It's difficult to tell who's a friend these days." His voice sounds hollow, like he's completely alone.

I can't help it, I stare at him. The lost look in his eyes evaporates and he flashes a smile my way. "Oh, come on, Avery. You aren't that naïve. You have to know that people have ulterior motives. Not everyone is good and kind. If you thought that about Sean, you'd be in a ditch somewhere."

"Hey, he's not like that," I bite back before giving my words any thought. "Besides, being jaded is just as bad as being naïve. They're opposite sides of the same coin. They both mess with your perception of reality and you lose something, some part of yourself that's necessary." Well, damn. Listen to me being all philosophical when I'm half drunk. Who knew? I didn't even slur any words.

An odd expression crosses his face and he puts the glass down. Trystan's chair remains tipped back and he tilts his head to the side like he has underestimated me. His lips part like he's going to say something, but he doesn't. Instead, those dark lashes lower and he looks to the side.

I know that expression. I've conjured a ghost, I'm reminding him of someone, of something that somebody who's no longer here has told him. Trystan lets his chair slam down onto all four legs and leans in. He's close enough to me that Sean will rip his head off if he walks in now, especially because of the hostility between these two men. "It's not necessary, and the coin can't stay on its side forever. At some point it falls, and I'd rather be cynical than naïve any day of the week."

I laugh in his face. "You think I'm naïve? Are you mental? I'm a goddamn call girl, my parents are dead, and I'm engaged to Sean Ferro. There are no butterflies and unicorns in my hair, no ever-present smile on my face, so what makes you think you have the faintest idea of who I am and what I'm capable of?"

Our eyes are locked, and I refuse to break the stare first. He doesn't know me, and that arrogance—the way he assumes I'm some spoiled brat that doesn't know shit—is just wrong. "I'm not some rich brat from Long Island. You might think you know me, but you don't. You don't have the slightest clue what I've lived through, but I know what you've been through. I know that look on your face, I know we've been in the same depths of Hell. The difference between us is that I refuse to give up and you already have." For some unknown reason I purse my lips and blow a puff of air in his face.

Trystan flinches and backs up. His mouth is pressed into a firm line and I know he wants to tell me off, but something holds him back. The guy says nothing. Instead, he gets up and moves to another chair and throws himself into it so one leg is hanging off the side without giving me a second glance.

Damn, maybe I shouldn't have said that, but any guy whose constructed walls that thick has something going on. Behind all those suave smiles is a broken man. It's impossible to miss because we're the same, him and me. No wonder he doesn't get along with Sean. It must be like looking in the mirror.

Sidney watches the exchange in uncomfortable silence. When Trystan walks away, and his back is to me, I go to stand— to say something else—apologize maybe— but Sidney touches my arm and stops me.

When I glance over at her, she shakes her head, and then changes the topic of conversation. "So, have you ever stripped?"

CHAPTER 7

I glance at her out of the corner of my eye and smirk. "Yeah, it kind of goes with the occupation. Have you?" I feel Trystan look up at me, but he doesn't say anything. Sidney blushes furiously and tries to hide her face. I laugh and bump her shoulder lightly. "I have an idea, come on." I stand and grab her wrist.

Sidney squeals as I pull her to the back, "What are we doing?"

"Looking for the dressing rooms."

"They're back there," she points down a hallway, and I pull her along with me. "Avery, what are we doing?"

"We're going to strip. What else?" Okay, I might be a little more than tipsy because that came out totally wrong.

Sidney jerks her wrist away. "I'm not stripping in front of Trystan!"

"That's not what I meant!" For some reason I start laughing because it seems really funny. I can picture myself on the stage and Sean walking in. I think he'd kill everyone. When I manage to get control of myself again, I put my hand on her shoulder. "No, let's just grab some of their stuff and dance on the stage. It'll be fun, and I think we both need some fun."

We find a dressing room and put on men's shirts and denim short shorts. I grab a top hat and Sidney grabs a feather boa. We head to the stage from behind the curtain and Sidney is laughing way too much. Her face is still bright crimson and she's muttering the same words over and over again. "I can't believe I'm doing this."

When we step out onto the stage, I raise my voice. "Hey, Trystan, hit the lights." I hear him grumble, but the guy moves. A few seconds later some of the stage lights pop up so it's not pitch black, and then a spot light appears. It's so bright that I have to shield my eyes if I want to look for Trystan out there. "Thanks." No one answers. Great, now he hates me, too.

"He'll come around," Sidney says, reading my thoughts.

I turn and look at her, offering a half smile. I glance at our outfits. The large men's shirts cover the short shorts. I unbutton the bottom of my shirt and tie it under my boobs and tell Sidney to do the same. I expect her to protest, but she doesn't. Music kicks on from somewhere and I smile. Sidney and I dance together for a little bit. She's laughing and blushing like crazy. I tell her to slow down her moves and suddenly she's dancing like a goddess. It's awesome. The girl has no clue how sexy she is. Add the huge smile on her face and that long hair and no wonder Peter is crazy about her.

I stand there for a second, watching her dip her head back and sway her hips.

She giggles and looks over at me. "I suck at this."

"No, you don't. You're actually really good." I laugh with her and say, "Watch this." I head over to the pole and basically do the same dance. I feel the music pulse through me and don't care who's watching me.

Glancing over at Sidney, I see her swish her hair in a circle and copy the movement with her hips. She laughs and looks over at me just in time to see me grab the pole, and kick my legs up. I wrap my thighs around the cold metal and lock my ankles together, before releasing my hands, and hanging upside down. As I slowly slip down the pole I reach for the floor, and when my palms find a firm footing, I kick off the pole and land on my feet. I put my hands over my head like a gymnast and smile.

That's when I hear Mel's voice. "I leave you alone for a couple of hours and you start stripping?" I hear her heels hitting the hard floor as she walks toward us. "What the fuck is going on here?"

"Mel?" I shield my eyes and walk to the edge of the stage. Sidney stops dancing and Trystan stands up, ready to throw her out. I hop off and plow into her. Wrapping my arms around her, I say, "I'm so glad you're all right. I thought you—" My jaw tightens and I can't say the words. I can't tell her that I thought I lost her.

"Who is this?" Trystan demands. He folds his arms over his chest and looks back at the door where the others are still talking, and occasionally yelling.

Mel escapes my death hug and rounds on him, ready to tell him off. "Don't you go talking to me like I'm some…" Her jaw drops when she sees Trystan. Mel's caramel eyes widen and don't blink.

I poke her shoulder. "Mel, this is Trystan. He hates Sean."

"So do I," she mutters.

I say, "Yeah, well, then you guys have something in common."

Trystan smirks, and then clarifies. "Why is she here?"

"Because I told her to come."

Trystan sighs and looks up at the ceiling before running his hands over his head. "Great. Jon's going to kill me. No one is supposed to be out here but me and Sidney, and I told his bouncer to go home. I assume Sean's coming?" Trystan turns his gaze to me and I nod. "Great." He turns and walks away, flopping back down onto the chair.

Mel is gaping and pointing. "That's Trystan Scott."

"I know. Are you all right? What happened?"

She doesn't look at me. "That's Trystan Scott. Like, *thee* Trystan Scott. Here."

Oh my God. How cute. Mel is star struck. She stands there like a twelve-year-old, practically giddy. I look her over and don't see any gaping wounds. There's no blood, and her brain has obviously left her body. "Listen, tonight kind of sucked. Grab a drink and join us on stage when you get over your whole boy band crush."

"I'm not a boy band." Trystan glares at me with his mouth scrunched to the side.

I smirk. "Of course not."

Trystan's lips twitch as he tries not to smile, or curse me out—it's getting hard to tell which one. I walk over to our table and pour another shot for each of us, before walking it over to him. His long legs are sprawled over the arm of the chair like a surly teenager. I hold out the glass.

His dark eyes stare at the drink for a beat too long, but he finally takes it. "Just for the record," he says, staring at the floor, "I admire you." His gaze flicks up and he lifts his glass.

What changed? I'm not about to ruin it and ask him. Maybe he has rock star PMS. "Well, coolness." I smile at him, sincerely this time, and look at my shot glass. "And just for the record, I'm a total fangirl. Your music is awesome, plus you have guts. So, I guess I admire you, too." I lift my face so he's looking right at me. "Truce? Or is it too late?" I hold out my hand, hoping he'll shake it.

That smirk teases his lips into a full grin. "I couldn't hate the future Mrs. Ferro, not when it'll piss off Sean to know exactly how much I like you." He laughs, clinks his glass to mine, and downs his drink. I do the same and head back to the stage.

As I pass Mel, she's still staring at Trystan, muttering to herself. "Well, don't just stand there, go say hi." I smack her back towards him.

Mel walks over to him like he's made of magic, as if the illusion will disappear if she moves too fast. Her voice is uncharacteristically soft. "Oh my God—it's Trystan Scott."

CHAPTER 8

Sidney and I are laughing hysterically, dancing on the stage, each of us with a drink in hand, when I feel eyes on us. Mel's been blabbering at Trystan for the past half an hour, going on and on, rambling and poking him like he's a mirage. It's kind of funny. Nothing fazes her, but put a rock star in the room and she's gone brain dead. Trystan takes it well enough. He just laughs and pats the arm of the chair and tells her to sit.

Then, two things happen at the same time. Mel's spine straightens—I see her out of the corner of my eye—she's a curve of shadow. And then, the rigidness turns to mush and she falls. I stop dancing and stare past her—there are also more shadows moving in the back of the room—people that I didn't see before.

Trystan scoops up Mel and sets her down in his chair. "Avery, your friend didn't even drink anything." He looks up at me and then at the back of the room. "Hey, guys." Even with my hand shading my eyes, I can't see who's back there, not past the glare of the spotlight.

"Avery?" a familiar voice asks, walking toward me. "What on earth have you done to Sidney?" Peter Ferro, uh Granz, walks toward me quickly. I lower myself and hang my legs off the side of the stage. The room tips a little bit and I blink hard. Peter seems tense, and in that moment he reminds me of Sean. Damn, it's late. When is Sean going to get here?

"Nothing," I reply. "She asked about stripping, so we've been dancing." I grin broadly at him. "Ask her to show you what she can do with the pole."

Sidney giggles and nearly doubles over. Peter looks up at her. "Is she drunk?" Peter's head snaps back toward Trystan with a pissed off glare and he could easily double as Sean in that moment.

Trystan is fanning Mel, trying to get her to wake up. "Don't look at me. They're the ones that swallowed."

All of a sudden, Sidney starts laughing. It's way too loud, and she realizes that no one else thought the line was dirty, so she slaps her hands over her mouth and cuts off the sound. Peter rubs the heels of his hands over his eyes and sighs.

I feel sheepish. "I'm sorry, Peter."

"It's not your fault." He smiles up at his bride-to-be. "Come on, cupcake. Let's take you home."

Peter holds up a hand, and Sidney walks over to the edge of the stage. The way she looks at him is the perfect combination of lust and adoration. The emotion is so raw, so intense, that I avert my eyes and look at the floor. Peter's wearing saddle shoes, black on brown, and vintage from the look of them. She sits next to me, and then Peter reaches up for her.

She slips into his arms and he holds her like that, and walks to the door, whispering things that make Sidney giggle softly.

My head tilts to the side and I'm repressing the urge to say, *awh*.

There's a sweet smile on my face as the rest of the people come into view. One guy is tall and built, with dark hair, and bright green eyes. There's a wicked grin on his face as his eyes travel over my body. "Hey, stripper girl. I have some ones. Wanna have a fun time?" The guy that's with him slaps Green Eyes in the back of the head. "What?"

"Sean will kill you." As the man steps toward me, I see the resemblance. The dark Ferro hair and bright blue eyes, the lopsided grin, and perfectly smooth skin. He looks like a younger version of Sean. "I'm Jonathan Ferro. This asshole is my cousin, Bryan." He jabs his thumb at him. There's a girl behind him wearing a blazer and a blanket and not much else. She won't meet my gaze.

"I'm Avery Stanz. I'm—"

"She's my fiancée." Sean's voice booms from the back of the room. No one heard

him come in, but everyone turns to look at
him.

CHAPTER 9

I slip off the stage and rush at him, darting around empty chairs and tables. The strain on his face is horrible. I can't imagine what he's been through tonight, what horrors came flashing to the front of his mind. Without a word, I fling my arms around his neck while the others gasp and whisper.

I kiss his cheek and plaster my palms to the sides of his face, forcing him to turn his tired eyes on me. "Are you all right? What happened?"

There are dark circles under his eyes and the tension in his neck and shoulders makes his body feel like stone. Leaning in close to my ear, he whispers, "Not now." I stay there like that for a second, and then peel myself off of him even though every urge I have says to hang on tight and never let go.

Sean walks past me and glares at his brother. "Well?"

Jon steps up to him. Damn they look alike, but Jonathan doesn't have the fine lines etched into his face. "Sean, this isn't your concern."

"I see. So, you're going to piss away your future. Good plan."

Jonathan stiffens and gets in Sean's face. "Since when do you care?"

Sean laughs, but it sounds more like Jonathan shoved a stake through his heart. Sean doesn't reply this time. Instead, he shakes his head and turns away, taking me by the hand and leading me backstage. He yells over his shoulder, "Your decisions are as abysmal as the company you keep."

Someone yells something back, but their words don't carry. Sean's jaw is locked tight and he's barely breathing. Once we're back in the dressing rooms, he sits me down in a chair, kneels in front of me, and looks me over. "Are you hurt?"

Placing my hands on his shoulders, I shake my head. "I'm fine. Are you all right? What happened? I was so worried about you."

"Did they mistreat you?"

At first I'm not sure who he means, but then I guess he's talking about Trystan, Jonathan, and Bryan. Touching his hand, I smile at him. "No, of course not. Trystan was actually very nice to me, so was your brother—both of them."

"Pete was here?"

I nod. "So was Sidney. I'm fine, Sean. Mel's fine, except for the passing out part."

"Is she drunk?"

"Nah, she's got the hots for Trystan." I laugh once and smile at him, pushing a lock of dark hair away from his eyes. "He talked to her and she fainted."

That makes him grimace. "Seriously?"

"Yeah, apparently she's got a weakness."

Sean nods thoughtfully and then looks up at me. Our eyes lock and I can't help but notice the massive amount of worry in his. "Thank God that's her only weakness."

"What do you mean?"

"I have to tell you something." His voice sounds like he doesn't want to tell me at all. "The police know the woman found in my room was a call girl, and that she was killed with a knife—one stab in her side, and then another, fatal, slash across her throat." Sean's voice is so still and devoid of emotion. I know what he's trying to tell me, what he means, but I don't want to admit it.

Shaking my head slowly, tears form in my eyes. "No, she couldn't have—she didn't…"

"She did, baby." My breath catches in my throat and I lean into his shoulder as the tears start to fall. "Mel killed that woman and we need to find out why."

CHAPTER 10

Sean and I stay like that for what seems like hours. His hands run down the back of my head and smoothes my hair as he whispers soothing words into my ear. At first I'm not sure why I'm crying, but then the images float through my mind and I know. After everything Mel's been through—after fighting tooth and nail to climb out of the slum she grew up in, getting that scholarship, selling her body to pay the bills—it was all for nothing. She's back where she started. If the cops catch her, there's no way they're going to call it self-defense, not with the wounds Mel inflicted. The thought makes me cringe even more. What would make her so frightened that she'd respond that way? She had to realize that she was giving up everything the moment she drew the blade across the woman's throat. I close my eyes and hold onto Sean tighter.

"Do they think you did it?" I ask the question that I've been dreading. Everyone hates him, even his own family seems to have a distaste for Sean, but I can't see why. Jonathan stormed off, but from the look of things Sean was trying to help him, the same way he helped Peter. Why can't Jonathan see that?

There are more things at play in the Ferro family than I can see, issues that lay far beneath the surface. Even Peter, who for all practical purposes seems normal, is far from it. What the hell happened to them?

Sean's chest rises and falls in a steady motion as he holds me close. His voice is soft and strained. He kisses the top of my head. "You don't need to worry about me."

Fuck. "So they didn't clear you? They think you're a suspect?" Pulling back, I look up into his tired eyes. "How? You were with me the entire time." Sean presses his eyes closed and steps away, turning his back to me as if he's trying to hide the fact that he's losing his composure. "Sean, talk to me." I reach for his shoulder and touch it gently.

He doesn't shake me off, but he doesn't turn. Sean runs his hands over his face and speaks softly, making sure no one else could possibly hear. "I'm not a suspect, not yet, but close enough and it's because of Amanda."

A chill runs through me and settles in my stomach. The sensation is so horrible that I want to cry and I know that it's only a fraction of the emotion surging through Sean. I don't wait for him to look at me. Instead, I step around and look into his face. There's a glassy sheen on his eyes and he evades my gaze.

I say what I know, the thing that no one else realizes and the one thing that Sean is desperate to forget. "You're a good man, Sean. No matter what they say, no matter what they see." I touch his cheek and smile warmly at him. "You hide it so well that even you forget at times."

He touches my hand, smoothing his fingers over the back of it. "You scare me more than anything I've ever encountered, and at the same time, I love you for it. You see through me, Avery Stanz, down to my mangled soul, and you stay. Every time, you stay." Sean's voice is uncharacteristically soft and he closes his eyes for a moment, and presses my hand more firmly to his cheek.

I don't worry about shattering the moment this time. I'm sure of myself—and even more certain of us. I know what he needs, but I can't give it to him here, so I take his hands and pull him to a clearing backstage. Sean follows without protest. When I stop, I take his hands and slip them around my waist and place my hands around his neck.

We dance slowly, saying nothing, until Sean bows his head and rests it on my shoulder. We stay like that for a long time, occasionally stepping as if we're still dancing. It doesn't escape me that Sean is letting me comfort him. He's given up control for the moment and is relying on me to hold him together. This is so unlike him that it worries me. I don't know if he's growing emotionally or falling apart. Sometimes those things look identical.

A flicker of movement catches my eye when one of the curtains across from us stirs. I lift my gaze and see Jonathan standing there in the shadows, watching. Our eyes meet and I mentally beg him to leave Sean for the moment. I can't stand to see him hurting any more right now, because it doesn't matter what Jonathan thinks—Sean cares about him. The man would do anything for his brothers, I'm certain of it.

The anger melts off of Jonathan's face and he stands there a beat longer than he should, almost shocked. His lips part slightly and his hands, which were fisted, unclench and linger at his sides. Has he never seen his brother hurting before? Sean the invincible is weakened at the moment, no doubt reliving the hellish night his wife took her life.

Maybe the embrace, and the way he hangs his head, makes Sean seem more human, I don't know, but whatever the reason, Jonathan shrinks back into the shadows and disappears without a sound. No one else comes looking for us either. We stay like that for a long time, and don't break apart until we're ready to face whatever comes next, even though I don't think I'll ever be ready.

CHAPTER 11

Mel. This whole goddamn mess stems back to her and I need to find out what happened. I'd assumed she wasn't in the room after I found out that it wasn't her dead body under the sheet. There was no blood on her clothes and no indication that she'd done anything wrong. It seemed like Mel left the hotel when she found out what happened, the same way I did. If one of us gets caught and it gets back to Black, we're all screwed.

I don't want to believe that my best friend killed someone, but this is Mel we're talking about. I've seen her threaten people with knives and so it's no shock she used one on somebody. Actually, I was under the impression that she'd cut someone up in the past for messing with her, but that was a past life, way before I met her.

The question that's swirling in the back of my mind is why didn't she run? Even after stabbing the woman, she stayed and slit her throat. Why kill her? Self-defense is understandable and forgivable—this isn't. Mel's ruined her life, everything that she was running away from has come back in full force. She'll never finish college or have a career. She threw away her entire future and I don't understand why.

Sean agrees to find the bar and give me and Mel some space. I walk through the worn curtain and wander toward the stairs that lead off the stage. Mel is awake and talking to Trystan who seems to be a night owl. Does anyone sleep anymore? I feel like a zombie. I've been running on fumes for hours and I'm pretty sure I'll trip and smear my face on the floor in the next hour.

Mel is sitting in a chair across from Trystan. She glances up and beams at me, before lifting a finger toward Trystan. "It's really him."

I can't help it, I laugh. "I know. He caught me outside. I pretty much fell on him."

"You did fall on me, not that I minded." Trystan sits up slightly and glances around. I'm sure he's looking for Sean.

I roll my eyes as I fold my arms over my chest, and throw my hip out. It's a naughty look that my mother gave me too many times. "Are you picking fights, Trystan Scott?"

"Psh, no." He grins broadly, which contradicts his words.

I drop my arms and walk towards his seat. Trystan leans back and looks up at me when I sit on the arm of his chair. "Listen, Sean will skin you if you mess with him tonight. Do me a favor and leave him alone." I wouldn't have said it, but I don't think Trystan's a jackass. I'm guessing the disdain for the guy is coming from Sean, because I'm not feeling it the same way from Trystan. It's more like Trystan is reacting to something. It's hard to like someone when they hate you. I need to ask Sean what he has against the rock star, because he seems fine to me.

Trystan doesn't promise anything, but his gaze meets mine and his smile changes. The corners of his mouth lose that teasing grin and his gaze softens to something that resembles understanding, and maybe even empathy.

Without warning, he glances at Mel and slaps his hands down on his knees. "So, I'm guessing you two want to talk." Trystan jabs his thumb at Mel. "She's had a rough night. Go easy on her." Then he's gone.

I slip into his velvety seat and look at Mel. She looks picture perfect as always. Silence stretches between us and for the longest time neither of us speaks. When I can't stand it anymore, I blurt it out. "What happened? Are you all right? How can you just sit there and pretend—"

Mel points a manicured nail at me and her expression flashes from pleasant to furious. "Don't you dare act like you have a fucking clue about anything!"

I lean forward and my hands start flying while I speak, begging for an explanation. "Then tell me!"

"Don't pretend you care about me. If this didn't happen in your room, you wouldn't have even spoken to me tonight."

That's it. She pressed my psycho-bitch button. I fly out of my chair and I'm on my feet, screaming in her face. "Bullshit! That's total crap and you know it! You know what I thought when I went back to the room? I thought you were under that fucking sheet! I saw your hand laying there, limp and pale and I thought I lost you. I thought you were dead! So don't sit there and act like I don't give a shit about you!"

Mel is in my face with her lips smashed together, ready to verbally decapitate me when a deep voice cuts through the room.

"Sit down." It's Sean. We both glance over at him. He looks more disheveled than I've ever seen him. The tension that lines his face is etching deep groves into his beautiful skin. Sean has a drink in his hand and is walking toward us.

When neither of us moves, he growls again, "Sit." Mel and I comply, and avert our eyes.

Mel lets out a huff of air as Sean steps between us. He glares at Mel. "You have no idea how much shit I went through tonight for you. Avery's your friend, so stop acting like a child. You killed someone and we need to know why."

Mel is grinding her teeth and stiffens in her chair. She doesn't look at either of us and I know she doesn't want to talk. Her nostrils flare as she breathes and her nails bite into the arms of her chair. She finally looks up at Sean. "I have trouble believing that you'd stick your neck out for me."

Sean seems agitated. He rolls his eyes and knocks back the rest of his drink before slamming the glass down on the table next to Mel. She flinches when he does it. Sean is at eye level with her. His voice is deep and menacing. "I didn't do it for you, I did it for Avery. You've been watching her back, so I've been watching yours."

Mel doesn't like that answer. "You've been trailing me?"

"I've been watching. I watch everything, especially when it comes to her." Sean points at me. "I know things she hasn't said and I know things you haven't admitted. Tell her what happened tonight or I will, and I guarantee you that it would be better coming from you." Sean straightens and backs away, before taking a seat to the side.

Mel swallows hard and glances at me again. I lose my patience. "Oh, for the love of God, just say it. I liked you before, when I knew you messed with people. You've threatened Naked Guy on more than one occasion. I know you aren't Mother Teresa and never have been, so just tell me!"

Mel glances at Sean out of the corner of her eye, almost pleading with him. "This is a bad idea."

"Tell her," Sean demands in a tone that makes me shiver. One of Sean's brows lifts as he folds his arms over his chest and his icy eyes narrow at her.

Mel doesn't like being told what to do. Her eyes shift from side to side and she leans back and cracks her neck. After taking

a huge breath, she dives into a story that I
wish I never heard.

CHAPTER 12

My body tenses as Mel speaks. I'm afraid for her even though I know she survived. After Sean and I left the room, things spun out of control. Mel ordered her dinner and when there was a knock on the door half an hour later, she thought nothing of it. Mel yanked the door open without looking, and there stood a woman with her complexion and caramel eyes.

Mel explains, "She looked like a fucking twin. It was creepy. The chick was about the same height and weight, and—get this—wearing the same dress."

"That's weird." My face scrunches up because I don't like where this is going.

"No shit. So I'm like, 'What do you want?' She laughs and manages to get into the room, but I don't let her in very far. It was like she was looking for something." Mel shakes her head and bites her lower lip, thinking before adding, "So, she can't get past me. The woman thinks there are other people in the room. I left the TV on in the bathroom and the tub was filling. I planned on vegging and watching TV, eating dinner while I soaked. Anyways, the girl steps up to me and smiles this creepy, toothy grin and I feel a barrel press into my belly. The bitch had a gun. She's not two steps inside the room and she pulls a fucking gun on me. After that, things get blurry."

"Mel," Sean scolds.

"I'm telling the truth, white boy." Mel huffs and deep frown lines cross her face. "Avery, everything happened so fast. I went from having the gun in my guts, to ripping her hair out and rolling around on the floor. The bitch pulled my bracelet off, so I crushed the stone thinking Black would send her ninjas, but they never showed. So,

I realize I'm on my own and use my knife on the bitch. She had me pinned."

"You had a knife on you?" I sound stupid for asking, but where the hell was it?

Mel nods once. The normal smile that's on her lips is gone and her head hangs between her shoulders as she buries her face in her hands. "I always have it strapped to my thigh. When I'm doing it, I hide the blade, but it's still in reach—under the pillow or shoved into the side of the mattress. I take care of me. I always have." Mel glances up and doesn't blink. Her eyes are cold and hard, like she's emotionally shut down in order to tell me the rest of the story. "Before the bitch knows what happened, I stabbed her in the side. She starts muttering about something that makes no sense, after cursing me out."

"What'd she say?" Sean asks. "What were her exact words?"

"Her voice isn't panicked, it's creepy, smooth as glass, and she says, 'You have no idea what you've done, you little cunt. Everything was perfect, and now they'll all...' Her words get garbled and I can't understand her. Her face contorts in pain and she starts screaming. That's a horrible way to die, and with the amount of blood pouring from her like that, she was as good as dead. She started begging me, so I ended it. Then I grabbed my stuff and ran. They must have found the body when they brought in the food."

I can't breathe for a few seconds and Mel won't look at me. Sean is watching the side of my face, waiting for my reaction. A few things stick and I blurt them out. "Someone was trying to frame you for something else—otherwise why would that woman be dressed like you?"

"And?" Sean prompts, watching me closely.

"The bracelet didn't work. Either someone tampered with it or it never worked to begin with. Black says she checks them every time we check in, so that shouldn't be it." I glance over at Mel. "What do you think?"

When Mel glances up at me, I want to throw my arms around her and tell her that everything will be all right, but I know it won't be. "I think we're fucked. Someone was using me to get to you and they're doing it through Black. The problem now is that none of this will lead back to her."

"But the transmitter?" I ask, still not getting what they're trying to tell me.

Mel's brow is pinched with worry when she looks over at me. Her hand grabs at the hair on the sides of her temples and I hear the distress in her voice. "Avery, there was no fucking transmitter. When the cops look at the bracelet, they'll think it was junk jewelry. It won't lead back to Black, it'll lead to me."

CHAPTER 13

Sean isn't tense for once. Sometime while Mel was talking, his shoulders relaxed and he's sitting back in his chair like it's a throne. His lips are straight, there's no curve to the corners of his mouth. He stares straight ahead, lost in thought.

I'm still piecing things together and don't like the way the puzzle is forming. If someone was impersonating Mel, then what was she there for? It feels like Mel left pieces of the story out, but for the life of me, I can't imagine what they could be. I find myself staring at the side of her face.

Mel is leaning back in her chair with her neck resting, looking up at the ceiling. "What?" she finally snaps.

"Tell her," Sean suddenly says, and glances over at me. "I already told you that I'll tell her if you don't." Mel doesn't move. Instead she stiffens and seals her lips. "Avery—"

Mel darts upright. "I'll tell her! You don't say a word." Pain is painted all over Mel's face. "Someone's been screwing with you, right? Asia told me that you had her in your room one night—that something spooked you." My jaw drops. I'm about to deny it, but both of them give me a look that shuts me up. "Tonight, before everything went to hell, I got a text with a video attached. It was you. He said to come get it or he'd post it online. Avery, I was supposed to leave the room and you guys were supposed to be there. I didn't leave because I thought he was messing with me at first, and then I said I was coming but the food was supposed to be there. I figured he'd wait, so I didn't leave—I just told him I was on my way."

I blink at her. "Wait a second, someone told you they had a sex video of me and that they'd post it if you didn't come down, but you didn't go because you wanted dinner first?" I give her a shocked look and don't know whether I should yell and scream or hug her.

Sean glances at me. "There's another player, and you're his target."

I can't process what they're trying to tell me. I laugh and shake my head, like they're both nuts. "You think someone is trying to kill me?" What a stupid idea. I laugh too much and too hard, but when I look up, Mel and Sean are watching me. Neither of them thinks it's funny—they both believe someone is trying to hurt me.

I roll my eyes, refusing to believe it. "The guy was in my room when I was alone. Why didn't he do it then? And what would he have to gain? I have nothing and I'm a nobody. I have no family and no one loves me, except you."

Sean watches me with those dark eyes and terror drips into my stomach like acid.

It's because of him. Someone is trying to hurt me to get at Sean. Oh God. My jaw drops open and quivers.

Before I can say anything else, he scoops me up in his arms and holds me to his chest, crushing me with his strong arms. "I won't let them touch you."

CHAPTER 14

I sit with Mel while Sean tries to talk to his brother one last time. It doesn't go well. I can hear them yelling from where I sit. Trystan is back, looking like a spring daisy.

He arches an eyebrow at me. "What?"

"Are you nocturnal, or one of those weird people that thrives on two hours of sleep?" I'm slumped back in my chair with a nauseous headache, propping up my face with my hand. Otherwise I'd be lying on the floor, since it started to look comfy a few hours ago. Trystan looks uncomfortable and absentmindedly touches the ring under his shirt. I get it. "Ah, you're neither, which means you're mental too. Welcome to the club."

He chortles and presses his fingers to his temples and seems to relax again. No one speaks and I keep wondering the same question. I know I shouldn't ask it, but I do anyway. "Mel?"

"Yeah?" she says from the floor. Her arm is over her face and she's lying flat on her back.

"What'd it feel like?" She pulls her arm off her eyes and sits up a little.

"You don't want to know that for real, do you?"

I'm stupid. I nod. The thing is, if I had to defend myself, I wonder if I could. I'm squeamish around blood, so how could I inflict enough damage to keep someone from killing me? I wonder if it's like some other part of the brain takes over and that's that.

Mel sits up and puts her arms around her knees. "I knew what I was doing, if that's what you mean. The moment I saw her, I knew something was wrong—like way the fuck wrong. When someone threatens you with a knife, gun, or whatever—there's no time to second guess anything. It's you or them, and I'm not dying."

Trystan's eyes flick between us as we speak, but he says nothing. I wonder what horrors he's seen because he doesn't react to anything we say. He just sits there, listening, like he knows what Mel's talking about.

"But how can you do it? I don't think I could."

That's when Trystan speaks up. "There's something inside of you that will wake up if you need it. I hope to God that you never do, but don't doubt that it's there. Like Mel said, your body will want to act—to protect you. Don't think. Just do it, and you'll live another day."

Mel and I stare at him. There's a second where his words are frightening, but then I feel nothing but empathy for him. He must have learned that from living with his father. The guy beat the shit out of him when he was a kid. It was in the papers and all anyone talked about for a while. Trystan Scott is a beautiful, charismatic, and charming singer. Everyone who meets him, loves him. He doesn't seem to have a violent bone in his body, but he came from a bloody and battered past. There's more story there, things I'll never know, secrets he'll never tell.

I nod, and am saved from finding an answer when Sean appears. "Let's go. Jon can deal with his own shit." He glances at Trystan and seems like he wants to tell him off, but doesn't.

"Wait, what about Mel?" I ask, as Sean's leading me toward the door.

"She knows what to do. Don't worry about her. Come on, I have the jet waiting at McArthur Airport."

The jet? Where are we going? I know better than to ask, so I say nothing and follow him outside. There's a limo waiting. We duck inside and take off. Sean is still angry from whatever happened with Jonathan. He lets out a rush of air and says, "My brother's an idiot."

I smile at him, trying to lighten the mood. "Which one?"

Sean smirks and glances over at me, before wrapping his arm around my shoulders and pulling me to him. He kisses the top of my head and starts talking. "Jon thinks I abandoned him when he was a kid, but that's not what happened. Pete seems to understand better, but not Jon. He won't forgive me, and he acts like his childhood was hell and it's my fault. The guy has everything, including the family fortune, then he goes and does things like this. I could understand this behavior from Bryan or Trystan, but not Jon. He's got too much on the line and our mother isn't exactly forgiving. There are things he doesn't know." Sean sighs and stops talking. It seems like he's going to say more, but he doesn't.

"I wish I had a brother or a sister, even if we didn't get along. I envy you." Sean makes a sound of disbelief. "No, I'm serious. Having crappy siblings is better than having none. You're not alone. I am. Besides, Peter seems to have forgiven you. Jon will understand sooner or later."

Sean doesn't say anything, he just holds me tighter and stares out the window until the limo pulls up to a little jet parked on the tarmac. The lights glow softly from inside and the door is open with a staircase beckoning us to board. Sean takes my hand and leads me onto the plane. When I step inside, I don't know what to do. There are eight huge leather seats that look as if they spin around. There's a table, a bar, and a huge paper-thin television on the back wall. Everything looks pristine and has that new car, uh, new jet, smell.

"Sit wherever you like." Sean gestures for me to continue into the back by myself. He disappears behind a curtain in front and speaks to the pilot before returning. By then I'm sitting in the last row and looking out the window.

"This is weird." I'm on a plane—a really posh one—and without going through the airport or dealing with security. No one groped me as if my underwire could be used as a weapon. The TSA confiscated my cannoli once because it wasn't sealed. I think the organization has a serious pastry problem. As soon as Sean is seated, we're taxiing down the runway. No waiting.

He smiles at me, enjoying my amazed expression. "I'm going to spoil you to the point that you don't think anything is unusual."

"I don't think that's possible, but I don't mind you trying." A lazy smile lines my lips. It's nearly sunrise and I'm exhausted.

"Sleep. I'll wake you when we get there." Sean hands me a blanket and a pillow, and I snuggle up and before I can badger him about where we're going, I doze off.

CHAPTER 15

The constant vibration of the plane has stopped and roused me. Okay, it's more of Sean's fingers poking my ribs. "Avery, wake up."

I want to roll over and stay here. I must mutter something to that effect with an expletive on the end for emphasis, because Sean laughs and says, "You can't stay here. Come on." He scoops me up and I get a dopey grin on my face. He's going to carry me like a bride over a threshold. Internally I sigh, because he's the most awesome man alive, but it's short lived. Sean drops my legs so I'm upright. They slam into the floor of the plane and jar me awake. I thought he was going to drop me.

"Hey!" I rip my shoulders from his grip and spin around in time to see a light smile lace his lips. Damn it. Why does he have to look so beautiful? I bite back the slew of nasty things I was going to say and resort to something less insulting. "Asshat."

That makes him laugh, full dimples and all. Sean must be hysterically tired because that wasn't all that funny. "I'll wear your ass any way you'll let me."

My face flames red and I glance around, assuming that we aren't alone, and we're not. The pilot heard him, and whoever is standing in the open doorway of the plane. I punch his arm, which makes him laugh more. *Note to self, stop calling Sean an 'asshat.'* Apparently it makes him think about doing sexy things with my butt. Psh. What a child. The expression must cross my face, because Sean's blue eyes go wide.

"Did you just roll your eyes at me?"

"No, Mr. Jones," I answer sarcastically, "I'd never roll my eyes at you. Once I started, I'd just keep going and God knows they would have fallen out by now."

Sean's smile vanishes as he leans in close to my ear, "You'll pay for that."

"I'm looking forward to it." We're eye to eye, nose to nose, and a kiss apart. Sean is charged, like a huge magnetic field and it feels impossible to keep the tiny bit of space between us. As he breathes, the rise of his chest brushes against mine and shoots tingles through my body. A smug look crosses my face, and I tilt my head to the side and whisper in the most seductive voice I can manage, "Asshat."

His eyes darken and this primal look comes over his face, before he presses those lids shut. I want to kiss both of them and hold him in my arms, but the look he has says things won't be like that tonight— or today. I've lost track of time.

When his eyes open, there's a jolt that travels through me when that wicked smile lines his face. Sean raises his fist to his mouth and bites it for half a second and then gives me a gaze that makes my heart pound fast and furious. "Let's get your ass inside, Miss Smith, and I'll see what I can do."

Girlish giggles erupt from me even though I try to swallow them down. My emotions shorted out hours ago. My hands cover my mouth, but I can't stop. Suddenly I see Sean's hand fly and the next thing I know, he slaps my butt hard. My hands move to cover my stinging hindquarters and I turn to stare at him, gaping.

He grins, "What? I thought you wanted to stop laughing?"

Oh God. That makes it worse. More incoherent thoughts tickle my stomach, stopping only after Sean helps me down the steps from the jet. I stop abruptly and look around. There are tall rafters and, hay? "Are we in a barn? Seriously? We hopped in your private jet to hide out in a barn?" I must look bizarrely worried, because Sean is kind to me. Maybe he thinks my brain broke on the plane.

"It's a hanger."

I point to the corner, "There's hay."

"Yes, it's for the horses. Where else should I store the shipments when they arrive?"

I shrug and start giggling again. "I don't know, in a barn?"

Sean doesn't reply. Instead he grabs my arms and pulls me from the hanger and out into the open. "Smart ass."

"Ah, back to my ass again."

"Your ass is going to be sore if you keep talking about it."

"Psh, so is yours." Yeah, I have no idea what the hell I'm talking about, but it sounded good.

That makes him look over at me. Amusement dances in his tired eyes. "I look forward to it."

Oh, shit. It figures he'd be into anything and everything. Why didn't I keep my mouth shut? I change the topic. We've been walking through a field. The grass is knee high, and early morning sunlight makes the dead grass look golden. It's pretty, but it appears that we're going to walk on forever since there's nothing to see but grass and trees.

"Where are we?" Just as the question slips out of my mouth, I see a beautiful house. It's a log cabin with huge shimmering windows. There's a stream that runs behind it, cutting the golden grass in two like a long blue ribbon. My jaw drops at the same time that my feet stop. It looks like something from a ski magazine, and not one of the exclusive tailored penthouses where Sean Ferro normally resides.

"One of my homes." His voice softens, and almost sounds somber. "Come on. I'll show you around." We walk up to the front, and go up the steps to a wraparound porch. As Sean puts a key in the door, I survey the area. The view from here is breathtaking. I can see the clearing we walked through, the stream, a gleaming lake in the distance, and it's all nestled between mountains that look positively blue in the early morning sun.

Sean pushes the door open and holds it for me. It's almost like he doesn't want to go inside. My chest constricts as I walk past him and step into the cabin. I'm barely inside before I spurt out, "Wow."

My neck cranes back and I stare at rafters that are twenty feet or more above my head. One end of the cabin is made from glass—twenty feet of glass. It's insane. The view from the porch is nothing compared to the one from this huge window. I'm drawn to it, and slowly cross the cabin. The floors are dark, hand carved wood with a distressed finish. There's a state-of-the-art kitchen with butcher block counter tops and rustic cabinets, but I don't stop. The window is amazing. I pass a pristine white bed with a wrought iron canopy and velvety drapes that look soft enough to sniff. I bet they smell like the Snuggle bear. I'm totally smelling them later.

Stopping in front of the window, I look out and can't help but smile. But something is way off. This seems so unlike Sean, and he's barely stepped through the door. He's standing there with it open behind him, like he might bolt. Turning, I ask, "What is this place?"

Sean's eyes lock with mine for a moment, then he looks down and shakes his head. He steps through the threshold, and pushes the beautiful carved door closed without a word.

"Sean?" I'm worried about him. I've never seen him like this before. It's my Sean, but he's broken. Sometimes there are no words. I cross the room and throw my arms around his neck and hold him tight. To my surprise, he doesn't pull back, but he buries his face in my neck. I hold onto him for a while, the way I did at the club, and wonder what ghosts haunt this place. What was this cabin supposed to be?

CHAPTER 16

When Sean snaps out of it, he looks like his old self. His defenses are up and that stern expression is back. Crap. I want to coax him back out, but Sean has other plans. He explains, "I need time to think and no one knows about this place. If anyone shows up here, we'll know who's trying to hurt you."

"Where are we?"

"Upstate, in the Catskills." New York is broken into several parts, the three main sections are Long Island, New York City, and then that massive amount of land north of Manhattan that's called 'Upstate.' His reference to the Catskills is the only thing that gives me any idea of where I am. If he didn't say that, we could be anywhere between the City and Canada.

I nod, and memories from last night start to flash behind my eyes. Sean grabs my wrist and commands, "No, Avery. Stop thinking. I want you to lay on that bed and let every thought rush out of your head. I only want you to feel what I'm doing to you. I want to be the one that evokes your fear or rapture. For the next few hours, I own you."

The corners of my lips lift as I step up to him. "You'll own me for much longer than that." I wink at him and whatever restraint he had is gone. Sean scoops me up and carries me over to the bed. He looks down at me and I swear that there's no blue left in his gaze. Those eyes are so dark that they're nearly solid black. As his eyes rove over me, I feel naked even though I'm clothed. My heart beats faster, wondering what he's going to do.

"Where's your bracelet?" he asks suddenly, looking at my bare wrist.

"In Gabe's limo. I shoved it between the seats." A smile crosses my lips as I think about it. "Black is going to assume I'm stalking her."

Sean grins at me before leaning down and kissing my forehead. "Good girl. That should give us a few days if the issue originates with her. She'll think Gabe is protecting you."

"Uh, I think he is."

"No!" Sean's voice is fierce. His entire body tenses to the point he trembles as he yells. "No one is protecting you, except me. I don't want you to trust anyone until this is over—not Mel, not Gabe, not even my brothers—no one. Do you understand me?"

Touching the side of his face, I nod. "I understand." My words carry more meaning, and I wonder if he knows how much I understand. He lost everything before and failed to stop it. The death of Amanda fractured his life in a way that he was unable to repair. If Sean doesn't stop this lunatic from messing with me, it'll destroy him. The final pieces that hold him together will come unhinged and the monster lurking within him will be the cause of his demise.

Sean's body shakes with tension that borders on rage. I know what he needs and I want to give it to him. I press my lips together and say the words he has to hear. "Take me, any way you want. Use me, Sean."

Breathing hard, he looks down, watching me. The fear slips off his face and the part of him that frightens me emerges. There's no rational thought, no logic in those eyes. It fades to something carnal and out of control. Sean grabs my dress at the neckline and tears it in two. The sudden movement, the sound of the fabric tearing, startles me. Before I can blink, he's on top of me, ripping off my clothes and tossing them aside until I'm naked. My heart is pounding so hard that I'm sure that he can hear it. I don't have the nerve to look him in the eyes anymore, even though I want to. I focus on his chest, on the places I want to touch, but I don't dare. Not now, not when he's like this.

Sean straddles me, pinning me to the bed and rips off his belt. Quickly, he flips me over so I'm facedown and yanks my hands above my head. Within seconds my wrists are bound together and tied to the headboard. He leaves my feet untethered and I wonder if it's because he wants to or because he's changing. Sean is different now, isn't he? This isn't like the first time he did this to me. Besides, I volunteered. I knew what I was giving permission for this time. Maybe I'm the one who's changed.

I feel his breath in my ear before I hear his voice. "Stop thinking." I try to shove all the thoughts from my mind, but I kind of suck at it. Sean's hand comes down hard on my bare ass. The sting makes me yelp. "Say, 'yes, sir.'"

My lips curl into a defiant, smug, expression. "Yes, Sean."

His hand comes down again, stinging the other cheek. I gasp, and try to look back at him, but I can't see him very well. He's directly behind me and I can only make out his location. "Wrong words will get you punished, Miss Smith. I want you to say, '*yes, sir.*'"

An insane urge to defy him rouses inside of me as a smile creeps across my face. I mean, what's he going to do? Hit me again? I kind of like that a little bit. It makes my girlie parts tingle. I'd be good with another slap. So I chide, "Yes, Mr. Jones."

Sean lets out a little noise, like he can't believe I defied him again, but his shock is short lived. He takes a pillow and shoves it under my hips, before parting my legs. I have no idea what he's going to do, but I like it. Thrill rushes through my veins, making me tug at my restraints. I want to tease him and do everything I shouldn't. Maybe I'm as messed up as he is.

He holds my legs open wide and with that deep voice of his, gives me another chance. "Stop thinking."

I'm insane. "No." The word rings out like someone slapped a gong.

My ass is in the air, thanks to the pillow. I expect his hand to come down on my round cheeks again, but it doesn't. Instead his open palm slaps me between my thighs, stinging my most sensitive parts. The jolt startles me and I try to crawl away, but Sean holds my hips still. "Say it."

I bite my lips and feel his hand come down again. This time it brings tears to my eyes, but there's something else, too. I don't know how to describe it. My insides feel like they're on fire and I want to be sated. Am I as messed up as he is? He's spanking my pussy and I like it. What the hell does that mean? Before another thought can cross my mind, his hand lands between my legs again and I yelp.

Without warning, Sean slips a finger up into me and I gasp. He's quiet for a moment and then removes his hand and leans over my back, pressing his body to me. His face appears next to mine, lightly pushing my cheek into the pillows. "So, it appears that you have a rather deviant desire, since getting spanked makes you so wet."

"It does not. I—" before I can finish my lie, Sean shoves the finger that was inside me into my mouth.

"Suck." My tongue tastes the sweetness and recognizes my scent. I do as he says, and suck his finger until it's gone and I only taste Sean's skin. "Good girl. And remember, behavior that pleases me will be rewarded."

I like the sound of that. "Anything I want?"

"Yes, if you behave yourself. Up until now, I have to say, you've been rather naughty. I'd slap you again, but I think you actually like it, so onto other things."

I nearly whine, okay, beg, for him to do more, but think better of it. Crazy Sean sounds more composed than I thought he'd be, which is interesting. "Back to you being good—say, 'yes, sir.'"

I make a face into the pillow and mutter. "Yes, sir." Being bad is more fun, at least I think it is until I feel Sean's naked body pressed to my back and he's kissing me. Damn, he stripped fast. His hard length pushes against my butt cheeks as his lips find the spot on my shoulder that makes me melt. He's close to finding my slut button—the spot that makes me totally wanton—so I wiggle, trying to get him away from it, because I want to keep my mind and defy him just a little bit longer, and as soon as he finds that spot, I'm toast. I'll be begging him for anything and everything. Damn him. I think he mapped my body when I wasn't paying attention.

Sean holds me in place, inching his lips closer and closer to the spot on my back, while one of his hands dips between my thighs. He forces them open and lifts his head for a moment. "Do whatever feels good, baby. I won't force you. Not this time."

What? My mind snaps to full alert right as Sean dips his head and lands his sinful mouth on the perfect spot on my shoulder. I gasp and wiggle, trying to get him to stop for half a second before I go still. His lips are pressed to my skin, while his tongue strokes against me. My body writhes without my consent as the place between my legs goes from damp to wet. My mind fades and I feel—no, I want. Sean's fingers press between my thighs and up inside of me, making me moan. My hips buck, not satisfied with fingers as he kisses my back. I want him, and I start saying things that would normally make me blush.

Sean pulls his fingers out and lifts them to my mouth. "Lick them." I do as he says, closing my eyes, and enjoying the way my body responds to his voice, to his commands. His lips work the spot on my back and I suck on his fingers, imagining that it's his hard length dripping with come.

He lifts his head. "Good girl." When he pulls his fingers away, I pout, but the emotion is short lived.

Sean takes hold of my hips and pushes into my slick core, slow and hard. I moan and beg for things I should never say. He sounds happy, teasing me, pushing in slowly and then pulling out to his tip, before slamming into me again, deeper. I beg for him to pound into me, spank me, and anything else.

Sean sounds content, almost happy, when he whispers in my ear. "Tell me when to stop."

Before I can beg him to fuck me more, he's gone. His body leaves mine and his lips are suddenly between my legs. His hot breath makes my thighs tense, but Sean pushes them apart and licks my slick flesh with his tongue. Stroke after stroke, he stays there, pressing his fingers into me, licking and sucking. I have no idea what he's doing, but I'm screaming out his name begging him to take me. I need him, my entire body is strung tight, craving the release. Sean brings me to the edge and I think he's going to tip me over into ecstasy, but he pulls away two seconds too soon. I scream and thrash when he disappears. His warmth is gone and I'm begging him to come back.

"Sean, please…" my voice is so breathy, and so completely shameless. I'd beg him for anything, to make me come any way possible. I need him deep inside me. I beg him again, and he's back, lying next to me.

"Tell me what you want, baby."

"Make me come, please Sean. I want you inside me. Please."

Before anything else is said, I feel something cold slip between my legs. Sean pushes a toy deep inside and it starts to vibrate. I feel so let down that it's not him that I nearly cry. I want Sean. That's when things go a different direction. He lowers his head to between my thighs and returns to the spot he'd been licking and pressing his fingers to before. I tense when I realize where he is and what he's doing. His tongue licks behind the vibrator at the delicate skin, and then over—oh God. I shouldn't like that, but it's making me feel positively high. My hips slow as apprehension chokes me.

Sean notices and returns to the spot on my back, but keeps the vibrator between my legs. He kisses my slut button and my mind turns off. Just like that, all my thoughts vanish and I'm all animal again. My hips buck, trying to find release, but Sean doesn't move the toy or increase the speed. I whimper and beg for things that I didn't know I wanted.

Sean is on top of me, and I feel his hard length pressing against my back while he holds the toy in place. He whispers into my ear, "I know you want it. Tell me baby, and I'll do it. Tell me to fuck you like this."

I can't. Even though I'm writhing against him, I can't say it. His lips dip to the spot on my back and after a while he tries again, but I still won't admit it, so he does the unthinkable and backs away.

"No!" I thrash, trying to see him. The toy is gone, Sean's warm body is gone, and I need him. Every part of me is pulsing with need. I can't control myself and I know I want what he's offering.

"Then say it."

"I want you to fuck my..."

"Say it," he growls, his voice deeper than I've ever heard it.

"Fuck my ass." The words come flying out of my mouth and sound horribly dirty to me. I beg him over and over again, and I tell him that I want him inside of me in every way possible, now. Then I plead with him to come back and sate me. "Sean, please."

When I feel him return and press his body to mine, I moan loudly. I can't hide what he does to me, how crazy he makes me. The delicious swirls are lacing through my stomach and my thighs are clenching, hoping for his touch. Sean slips the toy into place between my legs and pushes it deep into my slick folds. His lips return, kissing that spot on my back until I'm thrashing and screaming for him to take me. I'm not afraid of what he wants to do, so when he presses his cock to my ass, I moan and press back. Sean slides his long, hard length into me, filling me in a way I've never known. He's slick and pushes all the way in.

I gasp at the sensation, at the tightness. There's not enough air and I don't think I can ever get enough of this man. It startles me how much I want this, how much I want him to take me and use me. Before I can think, I push back against him and wish that I could touch him. My body is in sensory overload. The feeling of his lips on my back, his cock inside me on one side and the vibrator on the other is too much. I can't hold it together and I scream out his name as I climax. My hips slam back into him over and over again until he cries out. I feel him stiffen and then go slack against me. His rapid breaths slow and he pulls out, and then removes the toy.

Kissing the side of my face, he asks, "Are you all right?"

I don't answer. Instead I say, "Untie me."

Sean swallows so hard that I can hear it. He's worried about me. Maybe he thinks that I'm going to run, or that my face is covered in tears and that I hated it. Either way, he frees me. I roll over and get up on my knees and look into his eyes. God, those beautiful, haunted eyes, are so worried. I press my palm to his bare chest and shove him back into the bed. "I can't believe you did that."

He avoids my gaze. "Avery, I'm sorry. I thought—"

I smile down at him. "And I can't believe I liked it. Next time you want me that way, you don't have to ask. I trust you, baby. I want to be with you, anyway you want."

He tries not to smile and it's the sweetest look I've ever seen on his face. "So, what now?"

"Now, I get what I want, because I'm a very good, bad girl."

The corners of Sean's lips pull up. "Yes, ma'am."

CHAPTER 17

After a quick shower, I ride Sean until I can't sit up anymore. That might not sound romantic, but it's what we needed. Sometimes life is rough and rough sex follows. Sean has claw marks down his chest and I nipped his nipple a little too hard. He's started calling me a vampire because I like to bite.

I'm laying naked in the bed, tangled in the sheets, watching him. I'm so tired, and feel so sated, that it's hard to keep my eyes open. I don't know how he sits there, working. There's a little desk, and he pulled out a laptop, and he's researching something. I watch him from behind lazy eyes, in his jeans and bare chest.

He must feel my eyes on his back, because he turns and looks at me. "Go to sleep, Stanz."

I pat the empty space next to me. "Come sleep with me, Ferro. Like actual sleep, not sexy sleep." I grin at him.

Sean watches me for half a beat, like he's considering it, but doesn't move. "I can't. I have to do this."

"Do it later."

He's typing, not looking at me. "But I want to do you later."

"So, you're boycotting sleep, now?" I push up on my elbow, and the sheet falls away revealing my breasts.

Sean glances at me and then sighs, before walking over to the bed and sitting next to me. He traces the pad of his finger along my breast, tracing the slope to the nipple. He smiles like he shouldn't and pulls up the blankets, before leaning back against the headboard. Sean strokes the hair away from my face, gently repeating the movement over and over again.

He looks out the window and then down at me. "I've never slept much, my love." He smiles sadly and kisses my forehead. "It's all right. You rest. I have plans for later."

I don't argue, mainly because his touch has put me in a coma. As my eyelids flutter, he smiles at me. I feel happy even though the day was horrendous, because I can see the affection in his eyes. Sean isn't hiding from me at the moment, and I hope he trusts me enough to stay that way.

CHAPTER 18

By the time I wake up, it's nightfall. Sean is standing in front of the huge glass window, fully dressed in tight jeans and a black sweater with those shitkicker boots, and his hands held behind his back. I watch him from my pillow, wondering what he's thinking about. Before I can move, he turns and looks at me. God, his face is beautiful. I smile at him, still groggy from sleep.

"Hey," I say, feeling a little ashamed of what we did, now that I can think more clearly. I pull the sheets with me as I sit up and pull my knees into my chest. My body is sore, but in a good way. The thought makes me think of Sean behind me, pushing into me, and the fact that I pushed back.

Sean speaks before the burn of embarrassment spreads across my cheeks. "Don't belittle yourself for what you enjoy." He stands in front of the glass with the inky sky and a spattering of stars behind him. Moonlight fills the window, giving Sean a faint halo. He always sounds so composed, so certain of who he is and what he wants.

I'm not like that. I haven't had the luxury to experiment and live the life that I'd wanted, but things shifted somewhere and now I'm here with this man. I'm too nervous to look at him, but I force my gaze up anyway. "How'd you react after you did something you thought you'd never do? Especially when you realized that you liked it?"

Sean slips his hands into his pockets and studies me. "How many lines did we cross, Avery?"

I smile weakly at him and wonder if he's going to dodge my question. "Several. I had a picture in my head of the way things would be, and this wasn't it. It's more savage and I'm shocked at myself, and maybe a little disturbed. What does it mean that I like to be tied up even though it scares the hell out of me? What does it mean that I like to scratch and bite you so hard that you bleed? Sean..." I shake my head. I don't want to continue the thought because I don't like the dark places it's leading.

Sean looks out the window again and then takes a steadying breath. "Things for me were probably the way you pictured your future. I had my wife, we were together in civilized ways, and then she was gone. It felt—" His voice becomes so tense that his words are choked off. Sean glances at me from under those dark lashes. "I crossed so many lines that there was no way back after that. An honest man doesn't use hookers. A good man doesn't overpower them and force them to his whims. I did. I learned how to pinpoint their fears and feed them so they were terrified of me." He's breathing hard, watching me, and I know he's thinking about something specific. The way his eyes travel over my body tells me that he never finished what he wanted to do with me.

My heart pounds harder and I no longer feel ashamed, but he's right. Once the line is crossed, there's no going back. I know what I like and even if I don't want to admit it to myself, I know I want him to do things to me—things that frighten me. "You're not done with me, like that, are you?"

He holds my gaze and shakes his head. "I want to be done with it, but it's still there. I still picture doing things to you." He tears his eyes away and looks back out the window. His lungs fill with air and it makes his body swell. "I'm sorry."

"Don't be." He whirls around and gives me a quizzical look. I shrug and say awkwardly, "I kind of like it." I'm afraid of what he'll think of me, because I hate this. It's not normal to want to be used and taken that way, but I do—if Sean is the one doing the taking.

"Avery, you don't have to pretend to—
"

"I'm not. Why do you think I'm freaked out right now? Everything you've done has thrown me off kilter, and instead of running the other way, I want more. What kind of screwed up person wants more?" I'm nearly in tears, because I know what this means. I've read my textbooks, I've studied. We're both totally fucked up and it's the blind leading the blind. We're both going to fall down a hole.

Sean starts laughing, and at first I'm horrified that he's laughing at me. When he gets to the bed, he rips away the sheets and pulls me to my feet and walks me to the window. I stumble along, letting him lead me, worried that his neighbors will see my naked body. Sean pulls me in front of him and then does the last thing I expect and pushes against my back, forcing my skin to the glass.

I gasp and try to shrink back, but he holds me there and whispers in my ear. "How does it feel?" My heart is pounding, my nipples pucker from the cold, and I feel like I'm being displayed like a piece of meat.

He presses his hips against my back letting me feel how ready he is. "Answer me, Avery. Tell me if you like this or not."

Swallowing hard, I look over my shoulder at him, and nod. "It's cold and wrong, and if you fucked me against the glass, I'd come in a second because we shouldn't do it—but I like it."

"Is that so?"

I nod again and try to wiggle away from him. My boobs are going to be frozen solid, plus I'm pretty sure I see people down there. "Sean?"

He doesn't release me. Instead he holds me in place, revealing every last inch of me to whoever is walking below. His lips find my neck and my tension eases. He whispers, "You want this, don't you? You want me to pin you to the glass and fuck you until you fall to your knees." I nod, but refuse to think about the repercussions, which Sean likes. "Don't think, just feel, Avery. Do what feels right and if this feels right, do it."

Before I can speak, he has his pants undone and I feel his hot dick slide across my backside before he shifts my hips and forces himself inside my wet folds. Sean has me on display as he pounds into me, harder and faster, while pressing me to the glass. His hands tangle in my hair and pull it back, so I'm looking up at the sky. Coils of lust build deep within me and travel through my body, making me gasp and beg for more. He pulls my hair harder and pushes deeper, forcing my climax to erupt in vocalized pleasure. I claw at the glass as my body clutches and releases Sean's girth over and over again.

I'm breathing so hard, and am still so enraptured, that I don't realize what I'm seeing at first. After a few steadying breaths, Sean pulls out and zips up. He keeps me pressed to the glass, he's not done with me yet, but the figure below is watching. "Sean?"

"Mmm?" His lips are on my neck with his body pressed firmly to mine.

"Someone's there."

Sean doesn't move. He stays there like he doesn't think anything is wrong, but the way his body tenses tells me that no one should be anywhere near here. "Can you see his face?"

"No, he's dressed in a dark coat and standing toward the tree line. I saw something flash a second ago, like a piece of crystal or something, and…"

Before I can finish talking, Sean jerks me away from the window and to the floor. I don't understand what's happening or why he did it until a loud noise bursts through the room. A scream rips from my throat at the same time that Sean throws himself over me, and the floor-to-ceiling glass window explodes into a million pieces.

H.M. WARD

COMING SOON:

THE ARRANGEMENT VOL 13

To ensure you don't miss the next installment, text AWESOMEBOOKS to 22828 and you will get an email reminder on release day.

*****

THE FERRO BROTHER MOVIE

Vote now to make it happen!
http://www.ipetitions.com/petition/ferro/

*****

This is a fan driven series-when fans ask for more, there's more.

Go to Facebook.com/HMWard and join the discussion!

*****

TURN THE PAGE TO READ A
FREE SAMPLE OF:

THE
PROPOSITION
Bryan Ferro

H.M. WARD

THE PROPOSITION
Vol. 1

The sky is clear except for a few white glittering stars. They're hung high out of reach, impossibly beautiful and distant. The air has that crisp fall scent, and I know there will be frost tonight. Dad would have covered his plants with plastic to get a few more weeks from their fragile lives. The tarp is in the basement, still folded, where he kept it. The pansies will freeze and fade. This is their last night in this house, as it is mine.

Pushing the swing on the back porch with the tip of my foot, I start it swaying again. Life is so fleeting, so meaningless. The hole that's swallowing me is relentless. I thought I'd cry more, but I haven't even been able to do that. The tears won't fall. Neil says it's because my father's death hasn't hit me yet, but it has. The weight of his loss is pressing so hard on my shoulders that I can't lift my face from the dirt. For all those years, it was just the two of us. He was always there for me. He saved me from incomprehensible misery and now that he's gone, I find myself back in the shallows, unable to escape.

My eyes sweep over the wooden fence, taking in the rotten boards. Things were tight and I knew Dad sacrificed for me, I just had no idea how much until now. My college bills, my car, and all the things I needed were paid for without a blink, but I never stopped to wonder where the money came from. Dad worked hard, so I assumed it was enough.

I was wrong.

There hasn't been enough for a long time, and I had no idea. He never said anything. When I came home from classes at the end of the day, he'd hand me a twenty and tell me to be a kid and go have fun. He said stuff like that all the time. It makes me wonder if he knew what was coming, but there's no way he foresaw this.

When I came home from class last week, I found him in the yard, face down in a pile of leaves. My throat tightens and I push away the memory. It's not something that I ever want to see again, but it lights up over and over again. My senses are overloaded. I can still feel Dad's cold skin and the weight of his lifeless body as I rolled him over. The texture of his tattered flannel jacket is still on my fingertips. The sound of my strangled voice crying out his name over and over again still rings in my ears. I never felt so afraid. For the first time in a long time, I am alone.

My phone is on the wooden swing and chirps next to me. I don't feel like talking. Silence has encased me inside a tomb of misery since that day. Neil stood next to me and held my hand until hours blurred into days. Neil didn't want to leave me alone here tonight, but I insisted. It's my last night in this house. I'll never step over the threshold again. I'll never catch the scent of my father's aftershave in his little bathroom. All the memories will be lost and it will be like he never existed.

The Story of Bryan Ferro

COMING SOON

BROKEN PROMISES

A Trystan Scott Novel

Read more about the characters in
this book:

BRYAN FERRO
~THE PROPOSITION~

*****

SEAN FERRO
~THE ARRANGEMENT~

******

PETER FERRO GRANZ
~DAMAGED~

******

JONATHAN FERRO
~STRIPPED~

******

TRYSTAN SCOTT
~COLLIDE~

MORE ROMANCE BOOKS BY

H.M. WARD

DAMAGED

THE ARRANGEMENT

STRIPPED

SCANDALOUS

SCANDALOUS 2

SECRETS

THE SECRET LIFE OF TRYSTAN
SCOTT

And more.

To see a full book list, please visit:
www.SexyAwesomeBooks.com/books.htm

CAN'T WAIT FOR H.M WARD'S NEXT STEAMY BOOK?

⭐⭐⭐⭐⭐

Let her know by leaving stars and
telling her what you liked about
THE ARRANGEMENT VOL. 12
in a review!

CPSIA information can be obtained
at www.ICGtesting.com
Printed in the USA
LVHW041040070419
613259LV00001B/24